# Count Your Money

## Money

### WITH THE

# Polk Street School

• A Polk Street Special •

# Count Your Money

## WITH THE

# Polk Street School

• • •

## Patricia Reilly Giff
## Illustrated by Blanche Sims

A YEARLING BOOK

*A special thanks to Anne Nesbitt and her Coleytown kids*

Published by
Dell Publishing
a division of
Bantam Doubleday Dell Publishing Group, Inc.
1540 Broadway
New York, New York 10036

ISBN: 0-440-40929-2

Printed in the United States of America

April 1994

10  9  8  7  6  5  4  3  2  1

CWO

*To Laurean Meyer*
*with love*

# Chapter 1

Richard Best zoomed across the back of the room.

He raced around Sherri Dent.

Sherri was watering Ms. Rooney's ivy plant.

He nearly knocked her over.

"Sorry," he said.

"Thanks a lot, Richard." Sherri stuck out her pointy tongue.

"Beast," he said.

Sherri reminded him of his older sister Holly.

A real pain in the neck.

Beast dashed up the side of the room. He headed toward the first window.

He could see Wayne O'Brien rushing toward the last one.

He and Wayne were shade monitors this week.

Beast loved to snap the shades up as hard as he could.

It was great when they flapped around the roller. They made a ton of noise.

He looked out the window.

He could see his best friend, Matthew Jackson. He was two blocks down.

Matthew's cat Barney was following him.

Every two seconds, Matthew would turn around and say something to the cat—probably "Go home."

Barney wasn't paying attention, though. She kept on coming.

Sherri marched along next to the windowsill. "Out of my way," she said. "I have to water the rest of these babies."

If Matthew had been there, he'd be making dopey Sherri Dent faces—pulling in his cheeks, raising his eyebrows.

"Watch out, Richard Best," Sherri said. "You in that scribble-scrabble shirt. Want this watering can down your neck?"

Beast took a step back. Sherri Dent was one tough kid.

He hated the shirt he was wearing. It had a bunch of lines all over it. The pockets were so long, they hung down almost to his belt.

He grabbed the shade cord.

He stood back.

"Go!" yelled Wayne O'Brien.

Beast let go.

He could just about hear Ms. Rooney over the flip-flap noise the shade was making.

"I hope everyone has seen what's on my desk," Ms. Rooney was saying.

Beast waited while Wayne snapped up the end shade. Then he took another look out the window.

Matthew was nowhere in sight.

He'd probably taken Barney back home.

Matthew was going to be in big trouble for being so late.

Beast went over to Ms. Rooney's desk.

Everyone was looking at a pile of stuff.

Great stuff.

Fat pretzels. Bags of popcorn. Lime green erasers that looked like jungle animals.

Other things were there, too. Skinny-minny bead bracelets and colored boxes.

Ms. Rooney was standing behind her desk, smiling.

"Is this stuff for us?" Beast asked.

"I'm selling it," said Ms. Rooney.

Jill Simon looked as if she were going to cry. "I don't have any money," she said. "Not one cent."

Beast didn't have any money, either.

He thought about Matthew.

Matthew would lend him some—if he had any. And if he ever got to school today.

Beast stood up on tiptoe to see out the window. Matthew still wasn't coming.

Maybe Wayne . . . "How about lending me a dime?" Beast asked.

Wayne shook his head. "I just have enough for ice cream."

Too bad, Beast thought. He had found a nickel with Matthew yesterday.

They had bought two huge gum balls.

They had chewed them all afternoon.

They'd been working on Matthew's birthday puzzle. Beast had given it to him. It had jungle animals with stripes all over it.

It was so hard, it would take them forever.

Right now, most of the class was dashing toward the closet.

Everyone was looking for money.

Kids were yelling back and forth.

"Lend me a quarter," Sherri asked Emily Arrow. "I'll be your best friend."

"I know I have a nickel in the back of my desk," said Linda Lorca.

Beast looked at Ms. Rooney.

She was still smiling.

He was surprised.

Ms. Rooney didn't like a lot of noise.

Usually she'd be clapping her hands by this time.

The classroom door opened. It was Mr. Mancina, the principal.

Everyone raced for his or her seat.

Suddenly the whole class was quiet.

"Very nice company manners," said Ms. Rooney.

"Terrific class," said Mr. Mancina.

Beast sat up as tall as he could. He wanted to see out the window.

Matthew's red hat was bobbing up and down a block away.

Mr. Mancina slapped his pockets. "I know I have money."

He pulled out a bunch of shells. Tiny gray ones. Two large orange ones. "How many for a pretzel?"

Beast kept watching Matthew. Matthew was crossing the street now, almost to the schoolyard.

"Two gray, one orange," said Ms. Rooney.

Mr. Mancina put the shells down on her desk. He picked up a pretzel, took a bite, and went out the door.

Jim, the custodian, came in a moment later. "I think I'll buy an eraser."

"Two grays," said Ms. Rooney.

Jim raised his shoulders in the air. "How about two whites?"

Ms. Rooney looked up at the ceiling. "How about three whites? I'm going to make a wonderful necklace for myself."

"Well . . ." Jim looked at the erasers. "All right."

He put down the shells and stuck an eraser in his pocket. Then he was gone, too.

The door opened again. It was Matthew, at last.

Ms. Rooney frowned a little. Then she started to talk.

"Once upon a time," she said, "there was no real money. People used what they had. If I needed milk, Emily might trade some for a couple of shells. It was called bartering."

Matthew slid in behind Beast. "What's going on?" he asked.

"I think we're studying money," Beast said.

Ms. Rooney smiled. "I think you're right."

# Chapter 2

**B**east's room was the worst mess he had ever seen.

Every dresser drawer was open.

He could hardly step over the junk on his floor.

His sister Holly came down the hall. "If Mother sees what you've done to your room . . ." she began. She put her skinny hands on her hips.

Beast hopped over an old train set. He slid on an old book with a missing cover.

Then he slammed the bedroom door.

Holly tried to push it open, but he was too fast for her.

He leaned against the door until she went away.

Then he sank down on the floor again.

Under his night table was an empty Krispy Oats box.

Not quite empty.

He picked it up and rattled it.

A few krispies swish-swished on the bottom.

He could hear the money, too. Two quarters, a nickel, and a shiny new dime.

Money for his mother's birthday, next Thursday.

He had been dying to spend it all week. He could see himself racing down to the A&P.

He'd buy a couple of licorice sticks, or maybe a pack of peanut M&M's.

He couldn't do that, though. He had to buy something spectacular for his mother.

More spectacular than Holly would buy.

He shoved the cereal box back under the table.

He wasn't even going to think about that now. He had to think about something else.

Today was Swap Day in Ms. Rooney's room.

They were pretending there was no such thing as real money—just like in the olden days.

Beast looked around.

He had to find something Ms. Rooney might use . . . something she'd swap for a pretzel.

Beast kicked at an old train set he had pulled out.

It hadn't worked in a year.

Ms. Rooney would probably hate it.

Then he remembered.

He fished through the things on his floor.

Where had that book gone?

He grabbed it up.

No cover.

Too bad.

Ms. Rooney loved books.

He picked up his homework. He kicked a couple of things under the bed.

He was down the stairs and out the door in two minutes.

Way ahead of Holly.

He poked his head back inside and yelled good-bye to his mother.

"Don't forget your lunch, Richard!" she called.

Holly was coming down the stairs.

He hated it when he had to walk to school with her.

He hurried back down the hall. He took his lunch from the table.

Holly came into the kitchen. "Richard left sopping wet towels all over the bathroom," she said.

"Sop them into your mouth," he told her. He started to laugh. He slapped his knee.

Holly laughed, too.

He waved to his mother, slammed the door, and headed for school.

He'd have to remember to tell Matthew what he had said to Holly.

Matthew would think it was a riot.

He saw Ms. Rooney at the end of the street.

She saw him, too, and waited. "Do you have something to trade?" she asked.

Beast nodded. "A book."

Then he looked down. No book.

"Uh-oh," he said.

Ms. Rooney shook her head. "You could trade some work."

"What . . ." he began. He wondered where he had left the book. In the kitchen, maybe.

"Let's see." Ms. Rooney looked up, thinking. "You could wash the blackboards, empty the wastepaper basket. I'll pay you a couple of shells. Then . . ."

Beast grinned. "I could give you back the

shells for something else. A pretzel or something."

Ms. Rooney tapped him on the head. "Right."

They turned in at the gate and went upstairs to Room 213.

He pushed open the door. The room was as messy as his bedroom.

Kids were running back and forth swapping all kinds of things.

Beast took the blackboard pail down the hall for some water.

When he came back, Ms. Rooney was holding up a necklace. "Who would like this?"

Beast put down the pail. The necklace was perfect for his mother.

Sherri Dent was just ahead of him. "That baby's for me," she said.

"How about letting me take it?" he asked. "My mother's birthday is in a few days."

"Not a chance," Sherri said.

Beast started to wash the blackboard. He

made dopey Sherri faces with the sponge.
They dripped down to the ledge.

When he finished the board, Ms. Rooney
gave him three gray shells.

He took the fattest pretzel he could find.

Ms. Rooney grinned at him. She held out
her hand. "Three gray shells."

Beast went back to his seat with the pretzel.

Matthew was tearing open his popcorn bag
with his teeth. "I swapped a box of my
mother's writing paper."

Up in front, Ms. Rooney ran her hands
through her puffy brown hair. "How are we
going to work in this mess?"

"Who cares?" Matthew said.

Ms. Rooney laughed. "Can you imagine
what it was like before people had real
money?"

Sherri Dent raised her hand. "Maybe that's
why people got together and made money."

"I think you're right," said Ms. Rooney.
"We could make our own money, but . . ."

"Who'd pay attention to it?" said Sherri.

"Not the A&P," said Wayne.

"Not the pet store," said Jill.

Ms. Rooney was nodding. "What happened years ago is that everyone in the whole country got together. They made the money in one place, and . . ."

"Everybody uses it," said Wayne.

Beast sighed. This was turning into a whole big lesson.

He turned around to Matthew. "How about swapping a couple of popcorns for a bite of pretzel?"

# Chapter 3

It was lunchtime on Thursday.

Beast was wearing his scribble-scrabble shirt again. He tucked it in.

Then he felt his jacket pockets.

Good.

He could feel his money inside. A dime from the cereal box.

He'd be able to buy his mother a good present with it.

He dashed across the schoolyard.

He could see Holly jumping rope on one side.

She could see him, too.

She'd probably tell their mother he was running in the schoolyard.

"None of your b-i-business!" he yelled before she could catch her breath.

He could hear footsteps behind him.

Matthew's footsteps.

He made believe he didn't hear anything.

He got ready, though.

Matthew was going to . . .

Matthew took a flying leap and landed on his back.

He landed hard—much too hard.

"Oof!" Beast went down on the ground. He could hardly catch his breath.

He could feel tears in his eyes.

"Stop," he tried to tell Matthew.

Matthew didn't pay any attention. He rolled around on top of him.

"Fight for your miserable life!" he was yelling.

Beast could feel a stone pressing into his knee.

A stick dug into his ankle.

At last Matthew stood up. "Hey, what's the matter?"

Beast didn't answer. He made believe he had something in his eye.

"Beast?" Matthew asked.

"Nothing," he answered.

Together they looked around for their stuff.

One of Matthew's pencils. Matthew's key.

Beast slapped his jacket pocket.

He turned the pocket inside out. Only a penny rolled out.

A dime was lying on the cement.

"It's mine," Beast said. "For money day."

"It's mine," Matthew said. "I heard it drop when—"

"Mine was shiny, the shiniest." Beast reached for it.

Matthew reached, too.

Matthew got there first. He picked up the dime, looked at it, and put it in his pocket. "It's really mine," he said. "I can tell by looking at it."

The bell rang.

Holly went past. "Look what you did to your new jeans," she said.

"Look what you did to your face," Beast said back.

Holly raised her hand up.

"Oh, it's your real face," Beast said. "I thought it was Halloween and you had on a mask."

Matthew began to laugh.

Holly wasn't laughing, though. Her feelings were hurt.

Beast took a quick step after her. "Hey, Holly Polly," he said.

Holly looked at him over her shoulder. She gave him a quick smile, then raced away.

Beast dug into his pocket.

He could feel a rubber band and a piece of squashed popcorn. No money.

Matthew had his dime. He knew it.

Matthew was walking along, sniffling a little.

Beast had never noticed that Matthew sniffled that much before.

"Listen, Matthew—" he began.

"It's my dime," Matthew broke in before he could finish.

Beast followed him across the schoolyard.

He listened to Matthew's sneakers slap-slapping on the pavement.

A million kids were pushing in through the big brown doors.

Matthew pushed, too.

Beast stood back on the steps.

He couldn't believe Matthew had taken his dime.

He'd be the only one in the whole class without any money.

Matthew slipped in between two kids. He didn't wait for Beast.

He disappeared down the hall to Room 213.

Beast looked down at his jeans.

His new jeans.

Now they were his new old jeans.

A big hole was in one knee.

A little blood was there, too.

Beast was the last one on the steps.

He thought about going home.

Upstairs, the classroom window banged up.

It was Ms. Rooney.

"It's Money Day!" she called down.

Beast could see Wayne O'Brien coming across the yard.

"Come on, Wayne!" he called.

Maybe Wayne would have some money.

They raced down the hall . . . stopped running to quick-step past Mr. Mancina's office . . . then slid into the classroom.

# Chapter 4

**B**east hurried into the closet. Half the jackets had fallen off the hooks.

He slung his scarf over an empty hook and dropped his jacket on the floor. He headed for his seat.

"Nothing on your desks," said Ms. Rooney. "No pencils, no books, no papers."

Beast tried to stuff his books into his desk.

There was so much junk in there already that nothing fit anymore.

He dropped his books onto the floor.

Ms. Rooney frowned a little. "Let's try to get organized quietly."

Ms. Rooney waited another minute. "Now," she said. "Take out your money."

Up in front, Dawn Bosco dropped about a hundred pennies and nickels on the top of her desk.

Emily Arrow clicked her teeth.

Beast knew what she was thinking.

Dawn Bosco had everything.

Beast leaned over Matthew's shoulder.

The shiny dime was right in the middle of Matthew's desk.

Matthew saw Beast looking.

He put his hand over the dime.

Beast sat back.

He couldn't believe it.

Matthew was his best friend.

Matthew used to be his best friend.

Matthew didn't even look the same anymore.

"Did anyone forget to bring money?" Ms. Rooney asked.

Beast half raised his hand.

So did Wayne O'Brien. Wayne's face was red.

He was turning out to be a crybaby, Beast thought. Crying over a little thing like forgetting a dime.

"I have extra," Dawn Bosco said. "Plenty of extra."

She marched down the aisle toward Beast.

She put one penny on top of his desk. She put another one on top of Wayne's.

"Thanks," Beast said. Dawn was a good kid. He looked down at the penny. It was an old brown one.

He poked Matthew. "Want to switch?"

Matthew sniffled. "Are you crazy?" he said.

"Want to hear something strange?" Ms. Rooney asked. "Hundreds of years ago, peo-

ple in Sweden used square coins. The coins weighed almost as much as you do."

"I weigh a lot," said Jill Simon.

"Today," said Ms. Rooney, "the world's biggest money is on the island of Yap, far away. Their money is like stone wheels."

Beast tried to make a wheel out of his own penny.

It rolled off the desk.

He swooped down to grab it up.

"Who has a penny?" said Ms. Rooney.

Beast raised his hand. So did a lot of other kids.

"Look hard," Ms. Rooney said. "What do you see?"

Beast looked hard. He could hardly see anything.

The penny was filthy.

Everyone else was raising a hand.

"I see a picture of a man," said Emily Arrow. "He has a skinny little beard."

"It's a picture of President Abraham Lincoln," said Timothy Barbiero.

Timothy Barbiero knew everything.

"It has the year," said Emily.

Beast's penny said 1984. No wonder it looked so old.

Dawn Bosco was shuffling through her pennies. "I have about a million years here."

Emily clicked her teeth again.

"It says, 'In God we trust,'" said Jill Simon.

Ms. Rooney nodded. "Excellent."

"On the back is a picture of a building," said Noah Greene. "It's the Lincoln Memorial."

Ms. Rooney nodded again. "That building is in Washington, D.C. It's a wonderful place to visit."

Noah was another one who knew everything, Beast thought.

They spent a long time looking at coins.

President Thomas Jefferson was on the nickel, and his house called Monticello. President Roosevelt was on the dime.

Ms. Rooney was smiling at everyone. "What does a coin buy?" she asked.

Beast raised his hand. He didn't wait for Ms. Rooney to call on him.

"You can put a penny into the A&P machine," he said. "You can get a piece of that round orange candy."

"That's true," said Ms. Rooney.

"You can't get much else," said Dawn Bosco.

"That's true, too," Ms. Rooney said.

Ms. Rooney went over to the closet. She pulled out a bottle.

It was huge—twice as big as the one they had used for the candy corn contest.

Ms. Rooney could hardly lift it.

She put it on the floor near the pencil sharpener.

"One coin may not buy much," she said.

"But put a bunch of coins together—a jarful of coins—and then you really have something."

"Enough for diamond earrings," said Dawn Bosco.

"Enough to run away," said Wayne O'Brien.

Ms. Rooney didn't say anything for a moment.

"I wouldn't run away for a million dollars," said Emily Arrow.

Beast wouldn't run away, either.

"Enough money," said Ms. Rooney, "for our class trip."

Beast looked up.

"Yes," said Ms. Rooney. "We are going to save our coins all winter. We'll think of ways to earn money. We'll save—"

"Like crazy," said Emily.

"Yes," said Ms. Rooney. "And then next spring the class will have enough money to take a wonderful trip."

Everyone was clapping.

Everyone was talking.

Beast didn't feel like clapping, though. And he didn't turn around to talk to Matthew, either.

Going on a trip was all right.

Losing your best friend was terrible.

# Chapter 5

It was after school.

Beast's mother was doing dishes again. "We need bread," she said. "Orange juice. Cornflakes."

"Don't worry." He shrugged into his jacket. "I can remember."

"Give him a note," Holly told their mother. "He can't even remember his own belly button." She was laughing, though.

Beast laughed, too. He took the money off the counter and dashed out the back door.

He walked to the store slowly. There wasn't much to do anyway.

Usually he went to Matthew's house after school—or Matthew came to his house.

Not today, though.

Today he and Matthew hadn't even walked home together.

Beast took a breath.

He didn't want to think about Matthew. Matthew and his dumb dime.

"A loaf of white bread," Beast whispered. "A thing of orange juice. Cornflakes."

He said it again as he crossed the street.

Easy. Easy as one, two, three.

Just as easy as tonight's homework.

It wasn't the regular kind of homework. Spelling or math or stuff like that.

Tonight he had to think about three ways to save money.

He had to write them down on a piece of paper.

He had already thought about the first way.
He had written it down, too:

LOOK ALL OVER
THE SIDEWALK.

Terrific.

If everyone in the class found a penny that way, or even a dime, that would be . . .

It was too hard to figure out exactly, but it would be a lot.

Maybe enough for a trip without even thinking about another way.

He crossed Linden Street.

Up ahead, he could see Wayne O'Brien.

Wayne was coming out of the A&P. He had a big bundle in his arms. "Hey, Beast!" he called.

"A loaf of white—" Beast said under his breath. He waved to Wayne.

"Want to come over my house?" Wayne asked.

Beast stopped to think. He had never been to Wayne's house.

He didn't even know where Wayne lived.

"We can figure out how to save money," Wayne said.

Beast thought about the stuff for the store.

Nobody had to have a loaf of bread in two seconds.

They wouldn't need the orange juice until breakfast tomorrow.

And . . . he stood still.

He couldn't remember the third thing.

"All right," he told Wayne.

He'd remember if he gave it a little time.

They walked along Linden Street for about five blocks.

It seemed to take forever.

"Hey, where do you live anyway?" Beast asked.

Wayne pointed.

Wayne's house was different from his.

Different from Matthew's.

It was tan, brick, and stuck together with a bunch of other houses.

Wayne pulled the key from around his neck.

"No one's home?" Beast asked.

He was sorry he had come all this way with Wayne.

When Wayne opened the front door, Beast could see it was dark inside.

"My mother works at the gas station," Wayne said.

Beast followed him into the kitchen.

He didn't know anyone's mother who worked in a gas station.

Wayne's kitchen was a mess.

Crumbs were all over the place.

Wayne pulled the milk carton out of the refrigerator.

He took a big gulp.

"Want some?" he asked Beast.

Beast shook his head. "I have to go soon."

"Come on," Wayne said. "Let's go in the playroom."

Beast wondered what a playroom looked like.

But it was just a plain old room. Messy.

Wayne turned on the television. "I can think better with the TV on," he said.

"Me, too," Beast said.

Wayne looked up at the ceiling.

Beast looked up at the ceiling, too.

"How about selling something?" Wayne asked. "That's a good way to get money."

"Sell what?" Beast asked.

"I didn't get to that yet." Wayne began to flip the TV channels.

He flipped so fast, Beast could hardly see anything.

Beast thought about being at Matthew's house.

Matthew's baby sister Laurie always made them laugh.

Sometimes Matthew's big sister Cindy made cookies. They were always a little burned.

They tasted good, though.

And Matthew's mother.

Matthew's mother laughed a lot.

"We could sell model planes," Wayne said.

Beast wondered where they'd get the model planes to sell.

Wayne stopped flipping. "Nothing good on now," he said.

Beast stood up. "I think I have to go to the store."

"I've got it!" Wayne said. "We could have a car wash."

Beast nodded a little. That wasn't such a bad idea.

"Do you think we could both put that down?"

"Sure we could," Wayne said.

Beast smiled at Wayne.

He was turning out to be a pretty good friend after all.

Then he thought about Matthew.

Beast stood up and said good-bye to Wayne.

He let himself out the front door.

Cornflakes. The third thing was cornflakes.

Beast began to run.

He'd have to finish up the saving money thing when he got home.

Right now it was almost dark.

# Chapter 6

**M**s. Rooney had a piece of chalk in her hand. SAVING MONEY, she wrote in large yellow letters.

Everyone was holding up a piece of white paper.

The class was calling out ideas.

Everyone but Beast.

He had called his *looking-on-the-sidewalk-for-money* idea out first.

"It would take forever to check out all the sidewalks," Matthew said.

"Matthew's right," said a couple of other people.

"It doesn't hurt to look," Sherri said. "Just in case."

Beast looked at Sherri. He couldn't believe it. That Sherri wasn't so bad after all.

Beast called out his second idea, too.

Saving up birthday money.

No one liked that idea. Even Sherri didn't say anything.

Beast looked over at Matthew.

Matthew was standing next to the pencil sharpener.

He'd been standing there for ten minutes.

He was sharpening his pencil.

When he started, it had been long and yellow.

Now it was short. Very short. Only the eraser was sticking out of the end of the sharpener.

Beast waited for him to turn around.

Matthew always made faces.

This time he didn't, though.

He just kept looking out the window.

He just kept turning the sharpener.

Ms. Rooney was so busy writing down ideas, she hadn't seen him.

Dawn Bosco stood up.

"Old coins are worth more than new ones," she said. "Maybe we could try to find some."

Beast looked down at his penny.

"It has to be very old," Dawn said.

Beast felt a good feeling coming on. "Hey," he said. "Mine is very old."

"Like 1940," said Dawn. "Like 1950."

Beast sighed. His was 1984.

Matthew leaned away from the pencil sharpener. "Like how much would they be worth?"

Dawn squinted at the ceiling. "Maybe a penny would be worth two cents."

"Two cents?" said Matthew. "Big deal. That would take forever, too."

"Well," said Emily Arrow, "I think we

should stop spending money on candy and ice cream."

"Yes," said Timothy Barbiero. "Put all our spending money in the bottle."

Jill Simon's mouth turned down. "I like to eat."

"Well, some of our spending money," Emily said quickly.

Wayne O'Brien waved his hand around in the air.

No one paid any attention.

Beast felt sorry for him.

Wayne's face was getting red.

Beast knelt up in his seat. "Call on Wayne?" he asked Ms. Rooney.

Ms. Rooney wiggled her finger at Beast.

That meant "Sit down."

"I have an idea," Sherri Dent said.

She didn't even raise her hand.

Before Ms. Rooney could tell her to sit down, she rushed on. "We could have a garage sale."

No one said anything for a minute.

Sherri's face was red.

Beast knew how she felt.

"Great idea," he said.

Sherri turned around. "Thanks, Beast," she said.

Sherri's face didn't look so bad when she smiled, he thought.

He looked across at Matthew.

Matthew was still watching the sharpener.

The eraser end of his pencil was crunching its way inside.

Beast remembered he had dreamed of Matthew last night.

It was a terrible dream.

Matthew and Wayne were best friends.

And Matthew didn't even know who Beast was.

Beast looked down at his desk.

He felt like crying. He felt like a big baby.

He swallowed. Too bad for Matthew.

"Great idea, Sherri," Linda Lorca was saying now.

And Emily Arrow, too.

Ms. Rooney nodded. "We can use the stuff we swapped."

"Get real money for it," said Sherri. She nodded as if she were the president of the world.

Beast looked over toward Wayne.

Wayne's face was red as a beet.

He was still waving his hand around in the air—so hard that everyone should see it.

Ms. Rooney didn't, though. She was telling them they could have the garage sale in the gym. "Next Monday," she said.

Wayne looked as if he were going to explode.

"Ms. Rooney," Beast called.

He pointed to Wayne.

Ms. Rooney nodded. "Yes, Wayne."

Wayne could hardly get the words out fast

enough. "Me and my best friend Beast want to have a car wash."

Everyone was yelling "Great idea!" again.

But Beast felt his face get red. He could hardly breathe.

*Best friend.*

He took a quick look at Matthew.

Matthew was looking down at the sharpener.

Beast couldn't see his face.

All he could see was that the pencil was gone and the backs of Matthew's ears were red.

# Chapter 7

**I**t was Monday, a rainy day.

A special day.

Today was Garage Sale Day.

And something else.

Today Beast was going to make up with Matthew—even though Matthew had taken his money.

It had been a terrible weekend without Matthew.

Right now it took Beast a long time to get to school.

He was holding his mother's purple flower pot on top of his head with both hands.

Bunched up inside was his father's old fishing hat.

And underneath that was his scribble-scrabble shirt.

Even his mother had said it was getting too old to wear.

Mrs. Clark opened the classroom door for him.

No one was inside.

"I think they're in the gym already," Mrs. Clark said.

Beast nodded. He was soaked from the rain.

He could feel drops of water running down the back of his neck.

He took the steps carefully.

The last thing he needed was to drop the flower pot.

Everyone was racing around in the gym.

Wayne was standing next to a statue of a horse.

He had made a sign: BEEUTIFIL HORSE 63¢.

Sherri Dent was holding a bunch of old pencils. The points were sharp, though.

"I'm doing a bargain table," she said. "A penny a pencil. Two cents if the eraser is new and flat on top."

Beast put the flower pot down. He pulled out the hat and the shirt. "Those pencils are all chewed," he said.

Sherri raised her shoulder in the air. "They still write."

Beast remembered he and Sherri were almost friends now.

"That's true," he said.

He thought about making a sign for his stuff.

He wondered how much he should charge.

But right now, he had to look for Matthew.

What would he say to him?

He practiced in his head.

Want to come over to my house? he'd say.

That was it.

He wouldn't even say anything about not being friends.

He looked around.

Matthew and Wayne were dragging a table across the floor.

"Great," Ms. Rooney was saying. She was holding about ten sweatshirts in her hand. "I cleaned out my closet last night."

She dumped them on top of the table. "Would you straighten these out?" she asked them.

She rushed off to help Emily with a stack of books.

Beast started to fold the shirts.

How could he say anything to Matthew with Wayne standing right there?

A moment later, a class banged into the gym. "We're here to buy," said Mrs. Clark.

Wayne raced over to his horse. "Horse for sale!" he yelled.

"Listen, Matthew," Beast said.

Then he saw something in Matthew's hands.

"Hey," he said, "isn't that the puzzle I gave you for your birthday?"

Matthew nodded his head. "We never got to finish it."

Beast opened his mouth.

"I guess we won't get to do it now," Matthew said.

Beast looked at him. How could he sell that birthday present?

"No. I guess we won't," Beast said. "Why don't you use the dime you stole from me? Buy back your own birthday present."

Then he went back to the other side of the gym.

He didn't even look at Matthew all morning long.

# Chapter 8

It was after school on Wednesday.

Ms. Rooney's class was in the school-yard.

"Isn't it a great day?" Ms. Rooney said. "Not one cloud in the sky."

"Perfect for a carwash day," said Emily.

Wayne crossed his fingers. "I hope we make a lot of money."

Sherri tossed her head. "We made tons at the garage sale. The jar is half full already."

Matthew came across the yard. He was dragging the hose behind him.

Timothy had a pail and a bunch of brushes.

"What did we forget?" Ms. Rooney asked. "Something . . ."

"I'm first in line," Mr. Mancina said. "I expect the best car wash of my life."

"Whoo," Matthew said. "Your car is clean now."

"Well," said Mr. Mancina, "it's pretty good after all that rain. But I want to keep on top of it."

Matthew began to run the hose over the car.

Everyone else grabbed sponges and mops and brushes.

They began to work.

It was hard work, Beast thought. All that reaching up over the top of the car.

All that bending over to do the wheels.

"Got to get the windows clean," said Sherri. "Those babies have got to shine."

"Looks like a great job," said Mr. Mancina.

He reached into his pocket and pulled out a pile of shells.

"No good," said Ms. Rooney, smiling and shaking her head. "This time we're going for real money."

Mr. Mancina slapped his pocket. "How much?"

"One dollar—" Ms. Rooney began.

"And twenty-five cents," said Sherri.

Mr. Mancina pulled out two dollars. "Do you have change?"

Everyone looked at Timothy Barbiero.

He was the best math kid in the class.

"One dollar," he said, picking up one of the two dollars. He looked at the other one.

He began to count on his fingers. "Four quarters in a dollar."

Noah leaned over his shoulder. "Ten dimes in a dollar."

Sherri Dent said, "A hundred pennies."

And Beast said, "A huge pile of nickels."

"Let's go with the quarters." Timothy counted out three. He gave them to Mr. Mancina.

Beast wondered if that was right.

Everyone seemed happy so he guessed it was.

He turned to look at Matthew.

Matthew was wiping a couple of drops of water off Mr. Mancina's car with his sleeve.

Beast wondered if they would ever talk to each other again.

Matthew had been hanging out with Timothy all week.

"Hey"—Sherri put her hands on her hips—"how am I supposed to dry these windows?"

Ms. Rooney clapped her hands to her head. "I know what we forgot!"

"Something to dry with!" said Emily. "We need a lot more than Matthew's shirt."

"Let me think," said Ms. Rooney. "I know what we can do."

Beast knew what she was going to say. He started for the big brown doors before she began.

"The leftover things from the garage sale," she said. "The sweatshirts—"

"That ratty old shirt you didn't sell," Sherri called after him. "It'll make a terrific cloth."

"Hurry!" yelled Ms. Rooney. "More cars are coming. Matthew, help him!"

Beast started to run.

He reached the classroom ahead of Matthew.

He opened the closet door.

He grabbed Ms. Rooney's sweatshirts and an old scarf of Timothy Barbiero's. He grabbed some other stuff, too.

It made a huge pile in his arms.

Matthew came into the closet. He took some off the top of the pile.

"My shirt," Beast said. He pointed to the purple flower pot on the shelf. "I shoved it inside."

Matthew reached up to the pot. He started to pull.

The pot began to topple.

"Watch—" Beast began.

Matthew grabbed it just in time. "Matthew zee Magician," he said.

Beast began to grin.

Then they looked away from each other.

They started down the hall. They were half-way to the stairs before the sweatshirts began to fall.

Beast tripped over one. He grabbed onto Matthew.

Matthew's pile fell next.

They heard the clinking noise together.

A shiny dime was rolling along the floor.

Beast's mouth went dry. The dime was bright, shiny.

"Where did that come from?" Matthew asked.

"I think it's mine," Beast said. He thought

back to the day he and Matthew had had the fight. "I thought the dime was in my jacket," he said slowly. "But I remember now. I put it in my scribble-scrabble shirt. It must have been there all this time."

# Chapter 9

**M**s. Rooney's class marched down the street. They turned the corner.

Beast and Matthew were the last ones to turn. They were slower than anyone else. They were pulling an old red wagon with the money jar.

Up ahead was the First City Bank.

"A bank is much safer for our money than my closet," Ms. Rooney had said. "We'll leave it there until we're ready for our trip."

Sherri Dent spoke up. "My father said we'll

get money from the bank to add to our money."

Ms. Rooney nodded. "Yes, it's called interest."

The wagon went over a stone in the street.

The money jar teetered.

"Whoa!" said Beast. He could see his dime jiggling on top of the jar.

After the car wash, he and Matthew had put the dime in the jar together.

Beast had said he was sorry about forty times.

Matthew had said he was sorry about forty times, too.

Still, Beast knew it had been all his fault. Matthew had never taken his dime.

Sherri Dent marched back toward him. She cleared her throat. "I have something for you."

Beast looked up.

Sherri was holding out the necklace. "I was

thinking about your mother," she said. "It's a great birthday present."

Beast smiled. "I still have some money. It's in a cereal box."

Sherri thought for a minute. "No," she said. "You're not as bad as I thought you were. Not bad at all."

Ms. Rooney opened the bank doors.

"Thanks, Sherri Perri," Beast said.

Now he had two presents for his mother.

Last night he had made a card. He had written in red:

MOTHER YOU CAN USE THIS FOR BARTERING.

YOU CAN PAY ME WITH IT TO DO THE DISHES.

He had put FOUR TIMES on the bottom.

Then he crossed the FOUR out.

Three times was enough.

He hated doing the dishes.

"What trip do you think we'll take with our money?" Emily asked.

"I hope it's Alaska," said Beast.

"Or the prairie," said Matthew.

Matthew grinned at Beast. "I know one trip we're going to take," he said.

Beast leaned over to listen.

"We're going to Mrs. Clark's class," said Matthew. "I'm going to use my dime to buy my birthday puzzle back."

Beast couldn't stop smiling.

Even if the kid wouldn't sell Matthew the puzzle, Beast still had the cereal box money.

He was glad he had saved it.

They'd take a trip to the drugstore. They'd buy another puzzle.

The bank man lifted the jar out of the wagon. "I guess you're going to take a wonderful trip with this," he said.

Sherri Dent waved her hand around like crazy. "I know a trip we can take," she said. "A terrific trip!"

Sherri went on talking about Lincoln pennies and Jefferson nickels. "Simple," she was saying. "We could go to Washington, D.C., where the presidents were."

Everyone was clapping.

Beast leaned back. He didn't care where they went.

He knew he'd have a terrific time anywhere.

# More About Money

| | | |
|---|---|---|
| Penny | 1¢ | On the front: Abraham Lincoln<br>On the back: Lincoln Memorial |
| Nickel | 5¢ | On the front: Thomas Jefferson<br>On the back: Monticello (Jefferson's home) |
| Dime | 10¢ | On the front: Franklin Roosevelt<br>On the back: Liberty torch, olive branch and oak leaves |

| Quarter | 25¢ | On the front: George Washington<br>On the back: Eagle |
| Half dollar | 50¢ | On the front: John F. Kennedy<br>On the back: Eagle |
| Dollar | 100¢ | On the front: George Washington<br>On the back: Great Seal |

Every coin tells the year it was made. And every one of them has the word LIBERTY.

Coins are made in places called mints. When our country was brand-new, there was no silver at the mint. How could the mint make coins?

George Washington, our first president, gathered up his silver plates. Workers melted them down to make coins for the new country.

You can tell where a coin was minted. If it was made in Denver, it will have a tiny D on it. If it came from San Francisco, it will have a little S. Philadelphia coins have a small P, except the penny, which has no mark.

Everyone likes to keep his or her money safe. If you tuck your savings away somewhere at home, you may forget the hiding place! It's much safer to keep your money in a bank. Anyone can start a savings account. The best part is that they will pay you to leave your money with them to use until you want it back.

# $TRIKE IT RICH

### with the Polk Street School

---

## A BOARD GAME

Directions

1. Cut out the playing board. Paste it to some cardboard. You may need help cutting!

2. Cut out the Turn Cards, 4 Game Pieces, and the Polk Street money. You can paste the coins to heavy paper or a cereal box. They will last longer.

3. Do you need more Turn Cards or money? Make your own.

$ ======================================= $

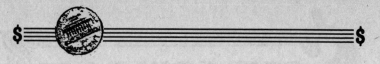

4. You can make the game harder. Change the numbers on the game squares.
5. You can even make up your own board game.

## MOST OF ALL, HAVE FUN!

To win the game, try to get the most money.
2, 3, or 4 people can play.

1. To start, pick a Polk Street person and put it on the Start square.
2. Each player takes 1 dollar bill, 2 quarters, 3 dimes, 3 nickels, and 5 pennies.
3. Draw straws to see who goes first. The player on his left is next.

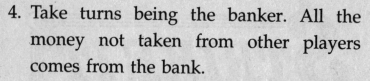

4. Take turns being the banker. All the money not taken from other players comes from the bank.

5. For each turn, a player takes a Turn Card. He reads the fun fact. He does what it tells him. When all the Turn Cards have been used, shuffle them. Use them again.

6. If a player runs out of money, she goes back to Start. She skips her next turn.

7. When the first player gets to the Finish square, the game is over.

8. The winner of the game is the player who has the most money.

You may need some help cutting out all the parts of this game and putting the game board together. Here is a picture that shows you how the board should look when it's finished.

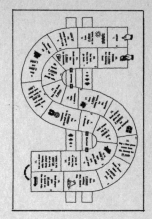

When you are cutting out the coins you can take a shortcut. Cut along the dotted lines instead of cutting out each coin.

---

EMILY

BEAST

MATTHEW

DAWN

People use yen for money in Japan.

**MOVE 2 SPACES.**

---

The first paper money was made in China.

**MOVE 3 SPACES.**

---

In England people use pounds for money.

**MOVE 6 SPACES.**

---

People use francs for money in France.

**MOVE 1 SPACE.**

---

People use rupees for money in India.

**MOVE 3 SPACES.**

---

In China people use yuan for money.

**SKIP THIS TURN.**

---

People use pesos for money in Mexico.

**MOVE 1 SPACE.**

---

Abraham Lincoln is on the 5-dollar bill.

**MOVE BACK 1 SPACE.**

---

Every dollar bill has its own number on it.

**MOVE 4 SPACES.**

On some islands in the Pacific Ocean, people once used feathers as money.

**MOVE 1 SPACE.**

---

Coins that are old and worn out are melted and made into new coins.

**MOVE 5 SPACES.**

---

The 100-dollar bill has Benjamin Franklin on it.

**SKIP THIS TURN.**

---

People use Canadian dollars for money in Canada.

**MOVE 2 SPACES.**

---

People used salt as money in Africa long ago.

**MOVE 5 SPACES.**

---

U.S. dollars are printed at the Bureau of Engraving in Washington, D.C.

**MOVE 4 SPACES.**

---

The first U.S. mint opened in Philadelphia in 1792.

**MOVE 4 SPACES.**

---

The ink used to make dollar bills is made from a secret formula.

**MOVE 3 SPACES.**

---

Long ago, people cut large coins into pieces to make change.

**MOVE 2 SPACES.**

**10 cents.**

**3.**
Sell a pretzel
to each player
for
**2 dimes.**

Ms. Rooney's
party.

**4.**
Give
**3 dimes**
and
**1 nickel**

**21.**
Noah returns
the
**2 dimes**
he borrowed.

**20.**
Spend
**5 nickels**
at the
garage sale.

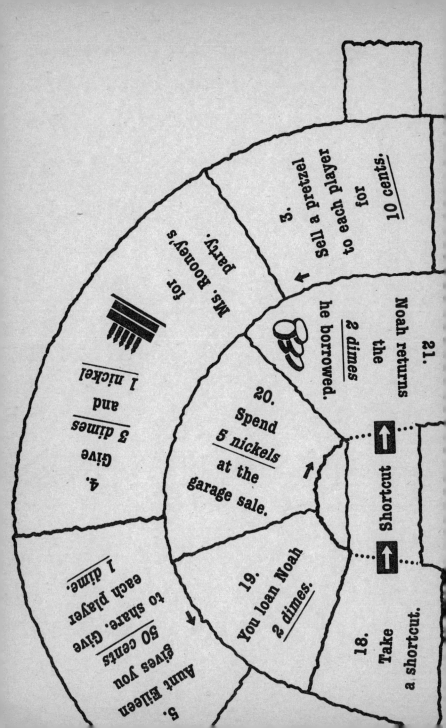

**Shortcut**

**18.**
Take
a shortcut.

**19.**
You loan Noah
**2 dimes.**

**5.**
Aunt Eileen
gives you
**50 cents**
to share. Give
each player
**1 dime.**

**6.**
Put
5 pennies
in the gum-ball
machine.

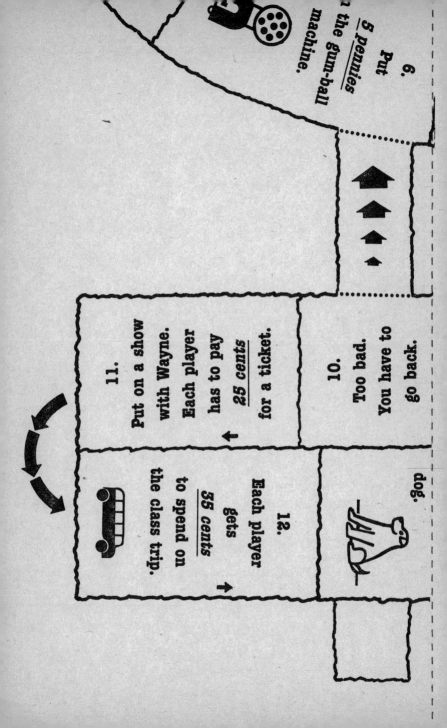

**11.**
Put on a show
with Wayne.
Each player
has to pay
25 cents
for a ticket.

**10.**
Too bad.
You have to
go back.

**12.**
Each player
gets
35 cents
to spend on
the class trip.

dog.

**16.**
Each player gives you _2 quarters_ for your birthday!

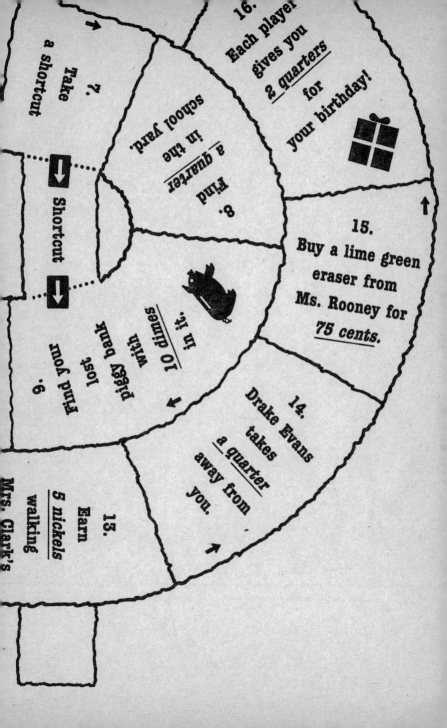

**7.**
Take a shortcut

Shortcut

**8.**
Find _a quarter_ in the school yard.

**15.**
Buy a lime green eraser from Ms. Rooney for _75 cents._

**9.**
Find your lost piggy bank with _10 dimes_ in it.

**14.**
Drake Evans takes _a quarter_ away from you.

**13.**
Earn _5 nickels_ walking Mrs. Clark's

START
1.

2.
Lose
*2 dimes*
at the beach.

23.
FINISH.
Get a *dollar*
for finishing
first!

22.
Too bad.
You have to
go back.

17.
Earn
*a dollar*
raking leaves
for Mr.
Mancina.

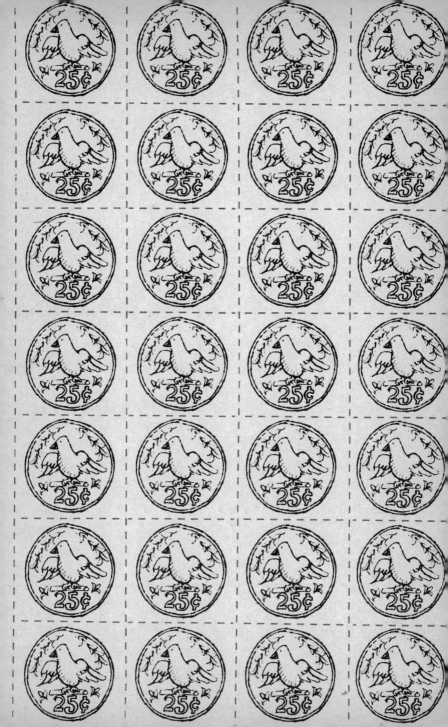

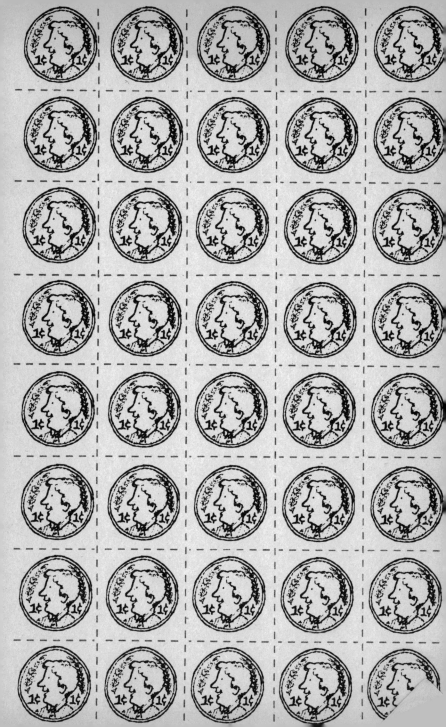